FEATHER
TALES

Petie Pelican

David M. Sargent, Jr., and his friends live in Northwest Arkansas. His writing career began in 1995 with a cruel joke being played on his mother. The friends pictured with him are (from left to right), Vera, Buffy, and Mary.

Dave Sargent is a lifelong resident of the small town of Prairie Grove, Arkansas. A fourth-generation dairy farmer, Dave began writing in early December, 1990. He enjoys the outdoors and has a real love for birds and animals.

Petie Pelican

By

Dave Sargent

Illustrated by
Jane Lenoir

Ozark Publishing, Inc.
P.O. Box 228
Prairie Grove, AR 72753

Library of Congress cataloging-in-publication data

Sargent, Dave, 1941—
Petie Pelican / by Dave Sargent ;
illustrated by Jane Lenoir
Prairie Grove, AR : Ozark Pub., 2000
p. cm.
PZ7.S2465Pg 2000
{Fic}21
1566763463x (cb)
15667634648 (pb)
Petie Pelican helps meek little Sherman Sheep correct
a mistake that he has made and develop self-confi-
dence. Includes factual information about pelicans.
Pelicans -- Fiction.
Sheep -- Fiction.
Self-confidence -- Fiction.
Lenoir, Jane, 1950- ill.
11865023

Printed in the United States of America

Inspired by

watching very interesting pelicans. They are proud birds. They hold their heads high. Maybe it's because they work hard for any food they get.

Dedicated to

all students who love to read about pelicans.

Foreword

Petie Pelican teaches meek little Sherman Sheep to have confidence in himself and to always do the right thing so he can hold his head high and be proud of who he is.

Contents

Petie Pelican

If you would like to have an author of The Feather Tale Series visit your school, free of charge, just call 1-800-321-5671 or 1-800-960-3876.

One

The Sudden Hail Storm

Big white fluffy clouds drifted along lazily in the azure blue sky. Petie Pelican looked at his twelve friends who were floating near him on the calm water of the bay. The weather, he thought, does not feel like springtime has arrived in the Gulf of Mexico. It seems like we just migrated from the north country a few days ago!

Petie stretched his huge wings. He flapped them in the air twice to get the attention of his flock.

"My fellow pelicans," he said, "the time has come for us to migrate northward for the summer."

"You're right," another agreed.

Murmurs and nods from the others told Petie that his instinct was right. And within moments, the very impressive birds were airborne. Their massive white and black wings flapped in unison as the flock flew in the military formation of a straight line.

Petie had never liked the idea of being in the lead. He much preferred following the group. Being very careful to stay out of the way of the others, he watched for his chance, then glided gracefully into the rear position. Not one pelican missed a beat—or, should we say, a flap of the wings.

For several hours, the birds flew northward without any problems. The terrain slowly began to change from sand to tall trees.

Suddenly the pelicans were hit by a strong wind. The air was cold, and a driving rain caused Petie to lose altitude. He gasped when he could no longer see his friends.

"Oh no!" he groaned. "I can't see a thing. The storm is too bad!"

He heard a rumble within the cloud, and then something crashed down upon his head.

"Hail!" he yelled, hoping that his friends might hear him and heed the warning.

All of a sudden the air was filled
with the icy stones, and Petie Pelican
was knocked to the ground.

Two

The Sheep Ran Away

"My, what a big bill you have!"

A meek little voice drifted through the fog in Petie's head.

"Wow!" the voice continued. "What a big bird you are!"

Petie opened one eye. A woolly white face was staring down at him, and he frantically tried to stand upright. The curly faced little critter started trembling, then backed up several paces. The pelican finally stood on his two webbed feet and tried to fluff his wet, muddy down.

He preened one of the more soiled
feathers with his massive bill.

Petie looked around and saw that he had fallen into a grove of trees. The storm had passed, but the air still felt cool to his bruised and slightly rumpled body.

"Who are you?" he asked the woolly critter. "And where am I?"

"My name is Sherman Sheep," the little fellow said meekly. "And this is Farmer John's place."

Petie slowly stretched one wing. "Good," he murmured.

Sherman asked, "You are glad you're on Farmer John's land?"

Petie ignored the question and stretched the other wing. "Great!" he shouted. "Neither one is broken."

Petie heard, "I'm glad I'm a sheep. Walking is safer than flying."

Petie glared at the little fellow, and the little lamb again backed away from the bird. The pelican felt bad when he saw a tear trickle down the woolly face and fall to the ground.

"I'm sorry," Petie said quietly. "I didn't mean to scare you."

"It's okay," the little sheep whimpered. He hiccuped and sobbed until his little shoulders quivered.

"Now, now," Petie said as he patted the little woolly lamb with one wing. "Everything is okay. I'll not glare at you ever again. I promise."

The little lamb looked up at the big bird and slowly shook his head.

"It isn't just you," he said in a humble voice. "I've had a bad day. Farmer John is going to shear my mama today, and I'm scared for her."

"Shearing is not a bad and painful thing," the pelican explained in a soothing voice.

Sherman Sheep looked at Petie and tried to smile. "It isn't?"

"No," Petie answered. "It isn't. Farmer John is just going to give her a haircut."

"Oh, I see," Sherman replied and slowly nodded his head.

Suddenly the poor little lamb began to cry. He cried as though his little heart was broken. He sobbed and bawled and whimpered. And, this time, Petie Pelican backed away.

Petie stood watching the heart-
broken scene for several seconds
before he asked, "What's wrong now,
Sherman? It's just a haircut, really.
Farmer John won't hurt your mama!"

"Yes, b-but . . . yes, b-but . . .
yes, b-but . . ." the lamb stuttered.

"Yes, but what?" Petie asked sternly. He was losing patience.

"But I told the flock to run away so Farmer John wouldn't hurt them!"

"I see," Petie said as he tapped one webbed foot thoughtfully on the ground. He crossed his wings over his back and paced back and forth.

"Hmmm," he muttered. "And did they do as you suggested?"

"Yes," little Sherman sniffled. "Every one of them except my mama ran away. I'm so ashamed!"

"No!" Petie shouted. "Never be ashamed! You need to correct your mistake, then hold your head high and be proud!"

The unexpected outburst from the pelican caused little Sherman to wipe the tears on his woolly leg, straighten his shoulders, and look wide-eyed at Petie.

"Okay, Mr. Pelican," he said in a strong voice. "I'm ready to correct my mistake. What do I need to do?"

"That's better. Now listen," Petie said. "I'm sure that my twelve feathered friends are grounded near here. We will get them to help us."

Three

Sherman Stands Proud

Petie Pelican watched Sherman scamper across the clearing toward Farmer John's farmyard. The lamb had a determined look on his woolly face as he disappeared from view.

The big bird smiled and quietly muttered, "I believe that little fellow is gaining confidence. Why, he's even looking a bit more proud!"

Seconds later, the pelican was airborne. After gliding over the woods and clearing several times, he saw a white object on the ground. He swooped low and watched one of his pelican friends motion for him to land. As his webbed feet touched down, six more of the flock ran toward him.

"Petie," one called. "Glad to see you. We thought you were lost."

"Come and help us," another cried. "Several are hurt from the hail stones."

Petie soon realized that some had bent feathers. Some had bruised bones. And some were embarrassed that they could not ride out the storm. But all in all, the entire flock was alive and ready for action.

Petie quickly explained little Sherman Sheep's problems. After a brief pause he asked, "Should we take time to help him?"

'Yes!" one pelican exclaimed.

"Of course!" another agreed. "I remember back when I was a young chick that I . . ."

"Never mind, Sophie," a deep voice growled. "We have heard all about your first diving lesson that about drowned you. Let's go look for those missing sheep."

"Good," Petie said. "I'm going to check on Sherman."

A few minutes later, the pelican saw Sherman scampering toward the shearing pen, but a sudden outburst of loud voices stopped him before he reached his mama. Petie landed near the corral where Farmer John and Molly were talking.

"Molly," Farmer John said grimly, "I can't find the rest of the flock of sheep. The wool buyer will be here in the morning for our wool, but, dadburnit, it looks like we aren't going to have anything to sell!"

"I just can't imagine what has happened, John," Molly replied. "Our animals know that we always take good care of them. Why would they run away?"

"I don't know," the farmer responded in an angry voice. "But if I find out what scared them, I'll put an end to that problem!"

Petie saw Sherman's little body start to tremble. The little fellow gulped, hiccuped, and groaned.

As Farmer John and Molly left the area, a voice beckoned the lamb.

"Pssst, Sherman! What's going on? I've been waiting to be sheared for two hours now."

"Mama!" Sherman whispered as he ran toward the shearing pen.

"Mama," Sherman said, "it's all my fault. But Mr. Petie is going to help me fix the problem, and then I can hold my head up high and feel proud!"

Petie walked over to Sherman and looked sternly down at him.

"If you do not help solve your problem," he said, "you will never feel proud. You know what you are supposed to do. Go now!"

"Yes, Mr. Pelican, I'm on my way. See you later, Mama!"

The pelican and Mama Sheep watched Sherman scamper away. Petie chuckled as the little lamb ran straight to Barney the Bear Killer and whispered in his long, floppy ear. The black and tan coonhound smiled and followed Sherman to the pig pen. Within seconds, the pigs were falling in step behind Barney. Finally the little lamb whispered instructions to the duck and goose, and they, too, joined the convoy.

As they entered the clearing, Sherman motioned for his followers to halt. The band of sheep were approaching with twelve pelicans following close behind. Petie smiled as little Sherman Sheep took charge.

Sherman carefully lined up the pigs to form a path to the shearing pen. Barney the Bear Killer was at the rear of the flock, while Sherman took the lead position.

Sherman signaled to the duck and goose, and they raced toward Farmer John and Molly's house. Honks and quacks echoed over the countryside. Sherman's little head was held high as he led the woolly band down the piglet alleyway. As the strange parade approached the shearing pen, Petie saw Farmer John open the back door and look out.

"What's going on?" he shouted.

Suddenly he smiled and pointed toward little Sherman and his woolly entourage.

"Molly!" he yelled. "Come here. Sherman has found our herd of sheep! Now we'll have wool to sell to the buyer tomorrow."

Petie winked at Mama Sheep, then turned toward his friends.

"We have a long way to travel, my friends," he said quietly. "And I think we are physically ready to move north. Besides," he added, "that proud little Sherman Sheep has everything under control here."

Petie walked over to Sherman and patted him on the head with one large white wing.

"Your pride in correcting your mistake is well earned, my little friend," he said. "We must go now."

Sherman bowed down on one knee before murmuring, "Thank you, Mr. Petie Pelican. I hope you have a safe journey."

"Thank you, Sherman," Petie responded with a smile. "Remember to stand proud. Goodbye for now."

As Petie Pelican took his flight position with the flock, he glanced back down at the little sheep. His woolly little head was held high, and he seemed to bounce with each step that he took toward the shearing pen.

I do believe, Petie thought, the little fellow has regained his pride. I hope he doesn't mess up again.

"And if he does," the pelican exclaimed, "I hope he doesn't just wallow in shame. No, I think he will solve the problem and feel proud. Won't he?"

Hmmm . . .

Four

Pelican Facts

Pelican is a common name for the species of a genus of large birds having a long, large, flattened bill, the upper mandible terminated by a strong hook that curves over the tip of the lower one. Beneath the lower mandible, a great pouch of naked skin is appended. The tongue is short and almost rudimentary. The face and throat are naked, the legs short, and the tail rounded. Pelicans may weigh up to 33 pounds, and the wings may span up to 10 feet.

GREAT
WHITE

Pelicans are widely distributed over most warm regions, frequenting the shores of seas, lakes, and rivers and feeding chiefly on fish. Pelicans have two very distinctive feeding methods. The brown pelican and the larger Peruvian pelican, considered a subspecies of the brown pelican, plunge-dive from the air into the water for their prey.

BROWN

FISHING DIVE

Most of the other species feed communally, swimming in an open circle in shallow water and driving the fishes into very shallow water where they snatch the fishes up.

PERUVIAN

FEEDING
YOUNG

Pelicans then store the catch in their pouches, from which they can bring it out at leisure, either for their own food or to feed their young.

Pelicans live in large colonies and build crude nests of twigs and branches near a body of water.

AMERICAN WHITE

The American white pelican, which breeds in the western part of the United States and Canada and winters east to Florida, is easily distinguished by its black wing tips. The brown and Peruvian pelicans are the only dark-colored species; their bodies are dark brown and their heads paler. Seasonal changes take place in the color pattern of the head and neck. There are four mostly whitish species with breeding ranges in southern Eurasia and Africa. One species, the Australian pelican, breeds only in Australia but wanders in winter to New Guinea, New Zealand, and other islands in the southwestern Pacific.

Scientific classification: Pelicans make up the genus *Pelecanus* and the family *Pelecanidae,* of the order *Pelecaniformes.* The brown pelican is classified as *Pelecanus occidentalis*, the Peruvian pelican as *Pelecanus occidentalis thagus*, the American white pelican as *Pelecanus erythorhynchos*, and the Australian pelican as *Pelecanus conspicillatus.*

J
Sargent